Adam's Christmas Eve

By
Patricia A. Knight

To businesswoman, Dallas Hutchinson, the suite at the St. Regis in New York City was an extravagant gift from a grateful corporate client. The resident billionaire was an unexpected bonus.

Theo Stockard's heart was well armored against a beautiful, charming, intelligent, sexy woman... or so he thought. To one of Forbes' Top Ten Executives of the Decade, the gorgeous blond standing in his suite was the classiest "gift" his friend had ever sent.

On one weekend in New York, two strangers experience the magic of Christmas in the most unexpected way.

www.trollriverpub.com
Adam's Christmas Eve
Copyright © 2016 Patricia A. Knight
ISBN: 978-1-946454-12-6

No part of this book may be reproduced or transmitted, with the exception of a reviewer who may quote passages in a review, without written prior permission from the publisher.

This is a work of fiction. All characters, names, events, incidents and places are of the author's imagination and not to be confused with fact. Any resemblance to living persons or events is merely coincidence.

ST REGIS
NEW YORK

Chapter One

"Welcome to the St. Regis, madam. How may I help you?"

Dallas Hutchinson returned the uniformed clerk's smile and slid her Texas driver's license and American Express Black Card across the hotel's marble registration desk. "I believe y'all have a reservation for me. I don't know if the booking is under my name or The Delta Group."

"Yes, madam. Thank you. Have you stayed with us before, Ms. Hutchinson?" He threw her a pleasant glance over the click of the keyboard.

"No, this is my first visit to Manhattan, actually."

While the clerk stared at his monitor and typed rapidly, Dallas brushed the plump flakes of melting snow off her cashmere overcoat and took in the five-star hotel's Rococo lobby of honey marble, gleaming brass, gilt crown molding and crystal chandeliers. The multitude of holiday decorations gave the imposing lobby a feeling of homey good cheer. With Christmas two days away, the muted background music of Nat King Cole singing "Chestnuts Roasting On An Open Fire" fit her mood exactly. She'd left behind seventy-eight degrees and clear blue skies in Dallas, Texas—not exactly a Hallmark Christmas card with the Budweiser eight-horse hitch prancing through the snow—but New York City was. Several inches of fresh white transformed the Big Apple into a winter spectacular, and the holiday vibe was just the therapy she needed to kick up her heels and be spontaneous.

The rectangle in her hand buzzed, and she eyed her cell phone hatefully. The Egyptians of the Old Testament had their ten plagues. In the United States of the New Testament, cell phones replaced the pestilence. She thumbed it off with a huff of satisfaction. She was going to *enjoy* the next two days.

"We have you booked in one of our Royal Suites for three days. Lovely choice, madam." The young man's voice conveyed rich approval. "The suite overlooks Fifth Avenue and 55th Street and features a formal dining room with full kitchen facilities and a living room with Central Park views. The Carrara marble bathrooms feature double sinks, a deep-soaking jetted tub, separate rain shower and toilet cabin, a bidet, and state-of-the-art technologies including mirror televisions and heated floors."

"My goodness." Dallas started laughing. "This weekend is a bonus from a grateful client. I didn't realize how grateful they were."

The young desk clerk grinned. "Obviously, extremely grateful. The suite comes with a resident butler, complimentary champagne, a free bar—"

Dallas raised her hand with a helpless chuckle. "Stop, stop. I'm overwhelmed. I have a butler?"

The clerk smiled broadly. "Part of our service, madam. You also have a chef-on-call." He slipped a key card across the white marble. "Enjoy your stay. Please don't hesitate to contact the concierge if there is anything you require."

~*~

She slipped her door card out of the suite lock and stepped into the warmly lit reception area of what passed as a suite at the St. Regis and was a million dollar apartment anywhere else. Her stiletto heels clicked on the marble as she walked past an overflowing flower arrangement on a sideboard in the entry hall. She placed her purse on its antique inlaid top and gazed around the living room with a sigh of appreciation. This was luxury. A white phone on a gilt-edged coffee table burbled softly, and she answered it on the second ring.

"Miss Hutchinson?"

"Speaking."

"This is the front desk. I'm so sorry to inconvenience you, but I booked you into an already occupied suite. I'm dreadfully sorry. The hotel changed computer systems for our reservations department last week, and it's been a complete nightmare. We've had your luggage sent to the Presidential suite, Room 3080. If you would please stop by the lobby and pick up another key card at your convenience. Again, I'm terribly sorry about the error."

"Not a problem." She placed the receiver in the cradle and retraced her steps to the entry hall, intending to pick up her purse and phone and leave.

"Well...hello there. I didn't hear you come in."

She turned in surprise at the deep baritone. *Sweet Jesus, Mary and Joseph!* Theo Stockard, President, and CEO of Stockard Investments, Ltd. and number one on Forbes Magazine's list of the top ten CEOs of the decade stood ten feet away, all six-foot-six, sandy-haired, blue-eyed inch of him attired in a closely tailored, charcoal-gray, business suit that appeared more bespoke than off-the-rack. The man was intensely private, stubbornly single and unrealistically gorgeous. Ever since she'd read the magazine's article on Theo Stockard and seen the numerous pictures of him, she'd entertained fantasies about the hard-driving executive.

"Are you the Christmas present Charlie sent?"

She'd always been a quick study. The possibilities flew through her brain in seconds. One: a female "present" sent from one male to another meant only one thing—sex. Two: did she want to have sex with Theo Stockard? Hell, yes! She'd never been shy about going after what, or in this case, who, she wanted. Three: What if the "real" Christmas gift showed up? Well, she'd deal with that issue when it arose. Somehow.

Dallas relaxed her straight spine as much as her lacing would allow and cocked her hip. "Yes. Yes, I am." Without any conscious effort, her voice came out low and husky.

He didn't move, but his expression warmed, and his gaze caressed her from head to toe in blatant admiration. "I didn't realize Charlie had such elegant taste in gifts. What's your name?"

She decided in a split second. "Eve. What's yours?"

His throaty laugh stirred her flutters into full-blown lust. "You mean Charlie didn't tell you?"

She shook her head slowly, a smile pulling at the corners of her mouth as he prowled to her and stood a hand's width away. She could smell the spicy, peppery scent of the cologne he wore, *Poivre by Caron*. As he lifted his hand to her face, she noted his clean hands and immaculate manicure. His forefinger gently traced her upper lip.

"Adam. For tonight, I'm going to be Adam." His blue eyes caught hers. "And you're going to be my Eve."

She'd barely whispered, "Okay," when his mouth descended and his lips brushed hers and then pressed into full, warm, gentle contact. Her eyes closed and she wanted to melt into him. She wobbled on her four-inch heels and placed her hands on his shoulders for support. His groan was almost inaudible. When he pulled back and her hands fell away, she felt bereft.

He cleared his throat. "Where are my manners? Let me take your coat."

He slipped her coat off her shoulders and laid it over his arm. Walking to the coat closet, he motioned to one of the sofas. "Have a seat. Would you like something to drink? We have a full bar. If you are partial to champagne, I have a very nice bottle of Krug Clos du Mesnil 2000 chilling.

She raised an eyebrow. If the man was going to offer her a $2,000 bottle of champagne, shoot, who was she to refuse? "I'd love champagne. Thank you very much." She sank into the overstuffed velvet cushions of the loveseat and crossed her legs.

From an antique mahogany tea cart doing duty as a bar, he selected a crystal flute and a heavy cut-crystal tumbler. With little ceremony, he uncaged and popped the cork on the *Krug Clos* that had been neck deep in a condensation-frosted silver ice bucket. Effervescence hazed the bottle tip as he poured her champagne. He set the champagne bottle down and pulled the cork from an imported bottle of Lagavulin 16. With casual ease, he splashed a finger's worth into the tumbler. Picking up both glasses, he crossed and sat at the other end of the loveseat. Inches separated them. She took the champagne flute from his offered hand.

"Not a champagne drinker?" She sipped the bubbly wine and, with soft laughter, wrinkled her nose as the carbonation popped on her nostrils. "That tickles. Mmm, this is delicious."

One corner of his mouth pulled up. He saluted her with the tumbler of amber liquid held between his index finger and thumb and murmured, "Give me a good single malt scotch." He raised the glass to his lips and sipped. His gaze never left her.

She leaned forward and put her half-emptied flute on the marble coffee table in front of them and uncrossed her legs. Toeing off her Kate Spades, she angled toward him and tucked her legs in their black patterned silk stockings under her butt; her corset held her backbone erect.

She loved her corsets. While working as a sexless professional in the corporate world, her corsets reassured her of her inherent femininity. The clasp of the tight lacing transformed her—if only in her mind—into a femme fatal of erotic titillation.

Curiosity about the course Theo Stockard...*Adam*... would take toward initiating their sexual activities nibbled at her. That she would spend the next few hours having sex with Theo was a given, but a man's approach to lovemaking with a woman conveyed great insight into his character, and she so wanted him to be different from the males in her past—the ones who smashed her against a wall and shoved their tongues down her throat the instant she said 'yes', or worse, made *her* take the initiative. There had to be some males left that weren't either awkward cavemen or emasculated metrosexuals.

"You confuse me." His even white teeth flashed a quick smile.

She cocked her head in question.

"I would never, for one minute, imagine a woman of your obvious sophistication to know Charlie."

"Perhaps I'm not the sophisticate you imagine."

He shook his head. "Cultured southern accent. Armani tag in the cashmere overcoat. Kate Spade pumps. Clive Christian perfume. God knows what you've got under that silk charmeuse blouse. Probably some sexy scrap of insanely expensive lingerie designed to drive men out of their minds. With your impeccable posture and tiny waist, I'd guess at a corset or waist-trainer."

Delight at his accurate assessment tickled her spine like the bubbles in the champagne. Her demi-bra, thong, under-bust corset and garters *were* wicked scraps of silk designed to seduce men. She reached for the flute and eyed him through her lashes as she sipped. His intent gaze never wavered. She placed her empty stemware back on the coffee table and fingered the top button on her blouse. "Should I satisfy your curiosity?"

To her surprise—and disappointment—he shook his head slowly. "My favorite part of Christmas was unwrapping my presents. We didn't have much, and there were never very many, so I examined each box from every angle, and never, never tore the paper. I drew out the mystery of the contents as long as possible. The reality of the gift was bound to be a letdown, my parents couldn't afford anything impractical, but at that moment just before opening the box…" he gazed at her with the eyes of a little boy alight with wonder "…in that moment, anything was possible."

Her nipples tightened into hard buds and pressed against the lace of her bra. When she dropped her hands into her lap, she pressed her forearms into her breasts to soothe the itch. Warmth soaked her thong in reaction to the pleasure.

He smiled as if he read her mind and knew of her body's response. "So…how do you know Charlie?"

Cautious alarm spiked through her. Having decided on this reckless action, she felt an intense desire to pull it off. A night in bed with Theo Stockard had made the number one spot on her fantasy bucket list shortly after she'd read his bio in *Forbes*. She could hear her heartbeat in her ears. The constriction of her corset shortened her body's requirement for more oxygen into breathy pants. "I've a confession. I've never spoken to Charlie. The arrangements were made through a …third party. My decision to be your gift was more or less spontaneous." She lifted a shoulder in a delicate shrug and discreetly studied his face.

He frowned and opened his mouth as though to ask a question, then halted. He shook his head with a rueful grin. "Doesn't matter. I've apparently made Santa's 'nice list' this year. Won't do to second guess Santa." He rose and crossed to the bar trolley and refreshed his scotch. He picked the champagne bottle out of its cooler by the neck and topped off her glass. "Give me a moment? I'd like to ditch the tie and jacket."

"By all means. Get comfortable."

He chuckled. "Until I get out of these trousers, that will be difficult."

"Oh." She cast her eyes demurely toward the floor, but not before seeing the prominent bulge straining the front of his slimly-tailored charcoal wool pants. *In another age, this is where I would fan myself and pretend maidenly ignorance.* As his long strides took him out of the room, she suppressed the giggle that rose at the thought and tossed back the contents of her glass. Rolling the empty glass in her fingers, she unfolded from the loveseat, moved to the ice bucket, refilled her flute and consumed that in a few swallows, too.

Phew. I need to cool off. She drew random doodles in the condensation on the bucket and then pressed her cold fingers to her neck.

Theo strolled back into the living room, tieless. The top two buttons of his shirt were open, and he'd rolled up his sleeves, exposing well-muscled forearms frosted with fine dark hair. He walked to her, leaned around to pick up his scotch and sipped from his tumbler. Six inches, perhaps, separated them. She wondered if he could see the rapid beating of her pulse. In her stocking feet, she was eye-level with his collar bone. His pulse was rhythmic and steady.

"Are you hungry?"

She lifted her head to look at him and shook her head slowly. "I don't want food."

He eyed her empty glass. "More champagne?"

She shook her head. "No more champagne. Thank you."

"Then I'm going to start unwrapping my present."

"Good plan," she whispered and swallowed at the wicked delight on his face. His fingers surrounded hers, and he escorted her several steps from the trolley with an almost formal courtesy.

"Stand here like a good gift, and don't move."

"Oka…"

"Hush." His lips grazed her mouth closed with a whisper. "My gift doesn't talk while I unwrap her." He held her gaze with a smile. When she smiled in return, he nodded and moved to stand at her back. Her breath made soft shushes of sound as it left her parted lips. She straightened and held her shoulders back, her breasts presented proudly. She couldn't have said why she did. It just *seemed* right. She loved the way he took command, and even though the man probably assumed she was a high-priced escort, Theo remained generous and careful with "his gift"—traits of a true gentleman. The tips of his fingers stroked her blond hair away from the right side of her neck. A warm kiss pressed into the tender junction of her neck and shoulder preceded the motion of his arms as they wrapped her and pulled her into him. His broad hands bracketed her waist and then moved gently up her ribcage until they rested just below her breasts. He chuckled low in his throat. "As I thought. Corseted. One more delicious layer to unwrap."

She felt the loss of heat as he stepped back from her. With two hands on her shoulders, he turned her to face him. His fingers rose to the buttons on her blouse and made steady progress unbuttoning them—a methodical stripping of each delicate disk through its buttonhole, pulling free the material she'd tucked into her skirt until her blouse hung straight around her and open down the front. Once again, she gazed at his collar bone. The rhythmic beat of his heart had increased.

Where her blouse had parted to reveal naked skin, his finger traced the mounds of her breasts shoved high by her demi-bra. "Judas Priest, Eve, you're making it very difficult for me to take my time."

Remembering his admonition not to speak, she grinned up at him, cocked her head to one side and moistened her lips, biting on the tip of her tongue before flicking it back in her mouth. Theo threw his head back and laughed. "Aww, shit…not helping." He clasped her head in both hands and kissed her, eating at her lips as if she was life and he a dying man. His tongue asked for entrance, and she opened, savoring the smoky flavor of the scotch he'd been drinking as his tongue teased hers. The warm peppery spice of his cologne added to the seduction of her senses and she gave up any hope of controlling her surrender. Drawing back slightly and lessening the pressure he applied to her lips, he took a shuddering breath and separated them a fraction of an inch, his forehead resting on hers. They both fought to steady their breath. She opened her eyes and glanced up. He stood, head down, eyes closed, breath gusting out of his open mouth. He straightened and dropped his hands. Amusement lit his eyes as he stepped back. "Note to self. No kissing until the package is unwrapped or I'll risk tearing the paper."

A low, throaty gurgle of laughter escaped her, and she shook her hair back. Her blouse opened wider. His eyes followed before he groaned and looked away.

Clearing his throat, he tapped her nose with a gentle forefinger. "No fair laughing at the overeager male. It's been awhile since the poor guy's gotten a present like this."

The corners of her mouth curled and she shook her head. "That's surely his choice," she whispered. "And there's no 'poor' about him. He's a gorgeous male. I'm certain he's had an abundance of presents in his recent past." Her right index finger wandered down the hard muscles of his chest, past his belt and delicately traced the ridge bulging upward to meet his waistline. She dropped her hands to her sides and suppressed a shudder of yearning.

He winced with a crooked smile. "You'd be surprised. His friends say he works far, far, far too much."

She caught her lower lip between her teeth and lifted her eyebrows with a cock of her head and thought, *you aren't working now*. He must have read her mind.

As if he traced the fragile wings of a butterfly, his fingertips lifted the edges of her blouse off her shoulders, and the garment slithered to the floor in a puddle of ivory silk. Gooseflesh ran up her arms, and her nipples pebbled tighter. She had to restrain herself from pressing her body into his. Desire flamed its way up her as if she were a matchstick. The provocative heat in his eyes added to her rapid burn. Holding the material of her waistband steady, he lowered the zipper on her skirt. With a slight shimmy on her part, the wool garment slipped down to her ankles. He swallowed heavily and murmured, "Step out of it."

She placed her hand on one of his broad shoulders for support and did as he asked. Surely anytime now, his restraint would abandon him, and he would fall on her and fuck her as she desperately wanted. She couldn't remember a time in her life when she'd felt more physically aroused. She couldn't recall a moment when she'd been made to feel more desirable.

He cleared his throat. "Now undo the garters and remove your stockings." As he watched, she flipped open the clips on the ribbons holding up her stockings and with her forefingers, slipped the sheer scraps of black patterned silk off her legs and straightened. He cleared his throat. "Turn around, please."

When she did, she felt his hands at the corset ties. Gradually, the garment loosened until it rested loosely on her hips.

"Face me again."

She did as he directed.

His fingers went to the hooks closing the front of her corset. They trembled as he started just under her bra and worked each fastener free. When—and with whom—had this man learned the technique for removing an expensive basque so as not to damage the boning? Dallas slapped down the small surge of jealousy. *You're Charlie's gift. Remember?*

Ultimately, the corset joined the blouse and skirt at her feet, and he stood with an unreadable expression on his ridiculously handsome face. The silence got heavy.

"Ermm…contents a letdown?" she whispered.

A wicked light filled his eyes and a lone eyebrow arched. He didn't speak, but his deep chuckle answered her question. *Okaay...not disappointed.*

His hands went to her bra straps and slipped them off her shoulders. With a long, slow exhale, he stepped into her. With one warm hand bracketing her waist, the other snapped the back of her bra open, and that piece of lingerie joined the growing pile of discards at her feet. She straightened. He stepped back with an unsteady inhale. Her nipples itched ferociously and she raised her palms and pressed her breasts together to sooth them. The sensation streaked to her plump clit and the slick flesh between her legs, and she choked on a sharp inhale.

"Stop. That's my job."

She dropped her hands to her sides, and her eyes slid shut on a soft moan when he cupped her breasts in his warm palms, pressed them together and strummed her erect nipples with the pads of his thumbs. She stood the stupefying pleasure as long as she could. "Oh, God…ah…I…" She opened her eyes. "Keep that up, and I'll come."

He grinned. "Isn't that the point of this entire evening?"

She laughed softly and breathed, "Won't you join me? Or do you just want to watch?"

He laughed and pointed down a hallway. "There's a big bed in the room at the end of that hall. Get in it. I'll join you in a moment."

She held him in a steady gaze as she stepped carefully over her pile of clothing and backed away a few steps.

"Eve?"

"Adam?"

"Ditch the thong when you get there."

With a crooked smile, she saluted, turned and padded down the hall, her feet making soft slaps on the dark hardwood floor. She felt his eyes on her, and she added a little extra to the undulation of her hips. Casting a look over her shoulder, she caught his gaze and murmured, "Please don't keep me waiting."

Chapter Two

Down pillows propped her in a partially sitting position in the vast king-sized bed. A silk top sheet loosely draped her naked body. She gorged on the luscious vision of a nude Theo Stockard, standing propped against the doorframe to the ensuite bath, half erect with an "I'm going to eat you, little girl" grin. *Damn.* If visual hunk-a-liciousness carried calories, she'd probably put on twenty pounds. A man with this combination of brains and body rarely crossed her path—never if her history was a guide. She'd had lovers who were smart, and she'd had lovers who were pretty to look at, but never both at the same time. *Please, please, God*, she prayed, *let him know how to use that impressive piece of equipment you've given him.*

With a silky prowl, he padded barefoot to the bedside and tossed an accordion strip of condoms on the side table.

She blinked slowly and watched the black and gold packages unfold to hang off the side. "I just love over-achievers."

Amusement lit his eyes. He reached for the sheet and slowly gathered the silk in his hand. The material whispered down in a slithering tickle, baring her torso a fraction of an inch at a time. When he'd exposed her completely, he sighed in satisfaction. "A natural blond. My favorite flavor. Spread your legs, please."

She complied with a sense of anticipation that became a yip of startled surprise when he lay on his stomach between her outstretched knees and opened them wider with the press of his broad shoulders. His face hovered inches from her carefully trimmed mound. His hands cupped her buttock cheeks, and his thumbs opened and exposed her most sensitive parts.

His brow creased in question at her soft yelp, and his blue-eyed gaze held hers. "No?"

"What? Oh! Yes! Good lord, yes." She waggled her hand. "Ah... please... Carry on."

No man had ever gone 'downtown' without some pointed hints on her part. She *must* re-evaluate her choices in boyfriends.

Her inner thighs, the creases where her legs met her torso, her abdomen—even the soft skin behind her knees—became targets of his attention, and she murmured appreciative encouragement. The flat of his tongue pressed a warm, gentle line of sensation from her opening to her clit in a repetitive stroke that had her squirming to lift her hips closer to the mouth doing such... insanely pleasurable things to her. Her murmurs became whispered pleas. Either he was a maestro at cunnilingus or she was hornier than she realized, because her orgasm built quickly. Some men in her past had complained that she took a lot of work to arouse. Evidently her body adored Theo. It was as if all her pleasure centers came alive at a single caress, or kiss, or trailing lick.

With broad thumbs that held wide the flesh hiding her clit, Theo bracketed the center of her pleasure and suckled. Her body stiffened as intense sensations close to pain slammed her into orgasm. Her wails echoed off the hardwood floors—closely followed by a male chuckle of satisfaction. Boneless lethargy followed the explosion of pleasure, and she lay motionless until the soft pulses between her legs faded.

Without moving, without opening her eyes, she croaked, "Give me a minute—or a year—to recover, and I'll return the favor."

Soft kisses covered the corners of her mouth, the tip of her nose, her eyelids. "Don't move. I've got this."

She sighed in appreciation... a man with a plan. God love 'em. She heard the soft crinkle of a condom package. She felt the bed depress between her widespread legs. Theo picked up her right leg behind the knee and pressed back, spreading her fully. If she'd had the energy, she would have opened her eyes and raised her head when she felt the pressure of his cock at her entrance. As it was, she simply murmured, "Umm, yes, please," and lifted her hips to offer an assistance he didn't require. In a practiced movement—she didn't want to think about that—he stretched and filled her to capacity, then released her right leg. There was a slight pinch as her flesh accommodated his and then his weight in the cradle of her hips drove her into the soft mattress. In an ageless response of woman to man, she bent her knees, wrapped his tight ass with her heels and held him deep within her.

"Okay, Eve?"

She nodded and her, "Oh…yeah," came out on a husky, low groan. She still couldn't summon the energy to open her eyes. "Go ahead. I can't come again this soon."

More kisses covered her mouth and cheeks. He propped himself above her on his elbows and in a gentle back and forth, rocked his pubic bone against hers. Spurts of pleasure at the pressure on her clit bubbled through her, but she knew from marathon sessions with her favorite vibrator she required at least ten minutes and some heavy clit stimulation before she could come again.

"I'll wait. Take however long you need."

Her eyes flew wide to find him inches above her face, his eyes half-lidded, the kisses he nuzzled on her, lazy and prolonged. "You're going to wait?"

He grinned and snuggled his chin into her cheek and jaw in a slow nod, nibbling from her chin to her ear lobe. "Mmmhmm."

"You're going to *wait*?" Well…what did you know? Theo was not only rich, handsome and well endowed, but he was also a member of an endangered species—a gentleman. He was going to be hard to walk away from.

His bemused look turned serious. "Any man who doesn't wait for you should be tossed out on his ass."

Did he really say that? She blinked several times.

"From the look on your face, you don't believe me."

"Well, it's just, um, most men—"

"I'm not most men."

"I'd say." Oops, did she say that out loud? She slapped a hand across her mouth.

He laughed at her expression of alarm, while his forefinger played in a curl on her forehead. "Thank you." His hips rocked a steady forward and back, his breathing even and controlled. "Believe me. I'm enjoying myself."

His hardness filled her and firmly stroked engorged tissue within her. The sensations produced were unfamiliar, but by no means unpleasant, and she wondered if she *could* come from just penetration. She never had before, but then… His hips maintained a steady rhythm as he scattered light kisses on her shoulders, neck and face. As minutes ticked by and his pace never faltered, he watched her with a smiling look of expectation. She felt miserable. She hated to disappoint him.

"I can't come from just... ah... just *this*."

"You sure?" His blue eyes sparked with mischief.

"Umm... yeah...?" She wrinkled her brow. "Oh...urm..." She wiggled beneath him. His cock kept hitting a particular place inside and the feeling produced was unlike anything she'd ... *Ah... that was good.* "Can you do that a little faster?" He grinned, changed his angle and stroked harder and faster. "Oh. Oh! Oh, God..." She swallowed hard and gripped his granite-like biceps. "I think I can come if you keep that up."

"That's the plan, darling. Let go for me."

She got lost in the rhythmic, regular stroke, and as her eyes widened in astonishment, she did.

With soft obscenities, Theo powered into her in a steady thrust that became increasingly irregular. Her cries had tapered off to whimpers when he buried his head in the crook of her neck, barked a curse, and came. His deadweight pressed her into the bedding, and she struggled to take a full breath. With a groan and a shudder, he rolled onto his back, tossing the condom into the trash basket by the bed.

For her, moving was out of the question. She lay, seconds from sleep, and marveled. She'd always thought the "G-spot" to be like a unicorn—magical and mythical. How nice to know she was wrong. She sniggered silently... or maybe Theo Stockard possessed a magic wand. Welcome to the twenty percent club—the club for women who could orgasm from penetration alone. A smile broadened on her face, and she chortled happily. With a supreme effort, she propped up on her elbows and snagged his bemused gaze. "Wow. I didn't know I could do that."

"I discovered, purely by chance, that many women just need a little extra time, something I'm happy to offer. One of the few benefits of getting older, I suppose. No more hair-trigger."

"What? Are you confessing there was a moment in time when you were less than the perfect lover?" She laughed at his grin and slow nod.

"Oh good god, yes."

"Well… however you got here…" She sighed in admiration and flopped back. "Don't change a thing."

"Hmm…" He looked at the bedside clock. "Eight-thirty. I could stand some food. How about you? Up for some dinner?"

All she'd had to eat that day were some mixed nuts on the plane, and now that he'd mentioned it, she was hungry and blissed out, and she'd kill for a deep tub filled with hot water and bubbles. "Yes, thank you. Something to eat would be lovely. I'll eat anything. Whatever you want will be fine with me." She paused. "If you don't mind, I'd love a bath."

He swung his legs around and sat on the edge of the bed, comfortable with his nudity. She could see no reason for him not to be. Glory, but he was a fine looking man.

"The bathroom is all yours. I'll call the chef and see what they can offer."

He made no attempt to hide his blatant appreciation of her body as she forced her wobbly knees to carry her into the bathroom. With a smile, she turned in the doorway. "If I'm not out in, say, forty-five minutes, I've fallen asleep—or drowned. In which case, please come rescue me."

He chuckled. "Will do. Enjoy your bath."

ST REGIS
NEW YORK

Chapter Three

With a smile that refused to diminish, Theo sauntered down the hall to the second bedroom's ensuite and did a quick once-over in the shower. He snagged an XL bathrobe out of the closet and walked back into the living room. The last couple of hours had been some of the best sex of his life. His smile broadened when he recalled the surprise on her face when he'd made Eve come the second time, and he allowed himself a moment of manly pride. Where *had* Charlie found this woman? She exuded a feminine vulnerability and honesty that all his business-sharpened intuition said was genuine. The thought that "Eve" was an escort struck him as highly improbable. She possessed too much class and lacked the hardness most "professional women" acquired. He knew something of those sorts. Early in the acquisition of his first million, he'd found a straightforward business deal with "working women" preferable to dating—a similar business negotiation, but containing hidden rules and agendas and far, far more expensive in the long term.

His hand was reaching for the telephone to order something from the on-call chef when the soft chimes of the suite's door bell rang. *Who's at my door at nine o'clock on a Christmas Eve?* His puzzlement compounded itself when opening the door revealed a young woman standing, hip cocked, balanced on six-inch, red, patent leather stilettos and a painted-on tube dress that started just above her breasts and ended just below her crotch. A string of blinking Christmas lights made a choker necklace and dangling earrings. She was pretty enough, but he'd never been overly fond of metallic latex, and her makeup appeared to have been applied with a spatula. Did natural hair come in that particular shade of Chinese red? The strong odor of *Giorgio* assaulted his nose. *Oh, God... not Giorgio.* The attack came seconds later. He sneezed violently.

"Bless you," she chirped with a smile. "You Theo Stockard?"

He nodded, pinching his nose to prevent another sneeze.

"Charlie sent me. I'm your Christmas gift." She grinned more broadly, straightened her posture and gestured outward with her hands. "Ta da!"

Two violent sneezes rocked him.

"Bless you. Bless you. What's the matter, honey? Allergies?"

He smiled through watery eyes. "Ah…yes, yes. Ah…tell Charlie that I appreciate the thought…" He had to stop to sneeze again. "But, ah…I'm not…ah, I'm not going to be able to…" Several more sneezes fired in rapid succession. He looked at her in helpless apology. "Sorry. Not feeling well." He began to inch the door closed. "Ah… Good night. Merry Christmas."

"Hey! Wait a minute." She stood taken aback.

In the midst of several more sneezes, he held up his hand and closed the door firmly, cutting off the source of the irritant. One arm outstretched, the other holding the bridge of his nose, he leaned against the door and waited for his sinuses to cease their hysterics.

He stood there, enduring the tearing eyes and the tickle in his nose, and then abruptly straightened. "If she's Charlie's gift, who in the hell have I just had sex with?"

His gaze fell on "Eve's" purse on the hall sideboard. Under normal circumstances, he wouldn't dream of violating the sanctity of a woman's purse. He'd had three older sisters who'd made that point with physical violence. These were not normal circumstances. He unzipped the bag and began removing its contents: a first class ticket, Dallas-New York-Dallas, a Christian Dior "Rouge" lipstick, Tic-Tacs, an engraved silver business-card case... he stopped at the business card case and flipped it open. It contained a black AmEx card, some folded fifties and... His eyes narrowed as he read. He tapped the thick, white, embossed card against the open case and slipped the card of *Dallas Hutchinson, CEO, Hutchinson, LLC., Dallas, Texas* into his bathrobe pocket. The next hour or so was going to be...interesting. Another thought occurred to him, and he rummaged through her bag and pulled out her phone. With a sour expression, he powered down the phone and looked around. He sighed, slid the phone to the very back of one of the sideboard drawers and closed the drawer. He'd already been a social media victim of supposedly 'candid' photographs taken à la Orlando Bloom. Once burned, twice shy and all that crap. Nobody needed their junk shared all over Facebook.

He tried to push back his stunning disillusionment and then mocked himself for being so easily conned. This wasn't the first time some woman had tried to entrap him, and normally, his gold-digger radar operated flawlessly. He'd whiffed on this one. His anger built in direct proportion to his disenchantment…and he had been enchanted by her. *Damn it all to hell!* With a deep sigh, he returned to the living room and slumped into the same loveseat where they'd begun the evening with such promise.

He rested his elbows on his knees and glared at the bar trolley. He was strongly tempted to grab the scotch bottle and forego the glass. His stomach gurgled hollowly. Well…there was no point in starving. Even a cultured, *conniving*, gorgeous, *gold-digging*, sexy-as-hell, *manipulative*, great-in-bed, *liar* needed to eat before he kicked her out on her delectable, natural blond derrière. He picked up the handset and rang the chef.

After a five-minute conversation, he replaced the phone in its cradle and listened to the happy hums of Eve…*Dallas*…in her bath. His anger drained from him, and he whispered every vulgar curse he knew. Knowing she had lied to him, knowing she was working some ulterior purpose, he still found it hard not to want the woman. Oh…he'd toss her out, alright… but she was one hella-sexy female.

His head fell back on the cushions, and he stared at the ceiling, his good mood as dead as analog TV. *This.* This was why he didn't date. This was why he made no room for women in his life. It was impossible to find a woman with integrity…someone honest. He'd yet to meet a female who wasn't working an angle—at least prostitutes were straightforward. Money for sex.

The phone burbled next to him. He eyed it with a snarl. "Stockard."

"Mr. Stockard, my apologies for disturbing you this evening. This is Andrew Mond, St. Regis Director of Concierge Services. I'm trying to locate one of our guests, a

Ms. Dallas Hutchinson. By any chance, would you know of her whereabouts?"

He straightened in his seat and crossed his legs, resting one ankle on his knee. "Yes, Ms. Hutchinson is with me. May I give her a message?"

The concierge cleared his throat. "If you would be so kind, I'd greatly appreciate it. This has been a poorly handled situation from beginning to end. When Ms. Hutchinson checked in this afternoon, there was a mix-up and the front desk assigned her your suite by accident. The bell service has placed her bags in the Presidential Suite, but she never returned to the front desk to pick up her key. I'm trying to locate her to tell her that the concierge desk will hold her key card. She can stop by with some ID and pick it up at her convenience. Oh! And if you would, please, let her know I *was* able to get her a ticket for *Hamilton* tomorrow for the 8:00 p.m. show. The seat is an obscured sight-line, but it's the best that's available. The show has been sold out for six months."

"Yes, I'll give her the message."

"Thank you, sir. I greatly appreciate it and have a happy holiday."

"Yes…happy holidays."

His smile grew broader and broader as he slowly replaced the phone and a similar expanding lightness of heart replaced his earlier disillusionment. "Eve" wasn't a scheming, opportunistic harpy. Her presence in his suite had been a mistake—not a plan. Did she even know who he was? For that matter, did he know who *she* was? Business cards could be printed to say anything.

He cocked his head and thought for a moment. He uncrossed his legs, reached for his cell on the coffee table and searched, *Dallas Hutchinson, Dallas TX*. He read every entry on a long list. Clearing his phone, he replaced it on the table, sat back and chuckled. *Damn.* He'd no idea why she'd had sex with him, but he doubted she was after his money. She had her own successful real estate development business—with an emphasis on the successful. While her net worth in no way approached his, she could retire tomorrow and never lack for a thing. *Aw... hell.*

So, she liked to play. He could play. It was Christmas, and he hadn't had a classy gift like her in a long, long time. It had been years since he'd done anything spontaneous. Hell, if he'd been willing to accept Charlie's gift—thank God Dallas had arrived first—why not chalk up this misunderstanding to some heavenly, fate-driven, opportunity of a lifetime? Why not make this a holiday to remember? *Good. Done.* He was going to allow himself some unapologetic enjoyment for the first time in years.

He wanted her to stay. He wasn't done with her. He'd figure out the whys and wherefores later.

ST REGIS
NEW YORK

Chapter Four

"I should never have indulged in that second helping of pie a la mode." Dallas looked at her corset still on the floor with the rest of her clothes and shuddered at the thought of lacing herself back into it. "Thank you for the lovely dinner."

Theo...*Adam*...stood at the bar trolley, his back to her, and poured himself an after dinner drink. He'd been charming during dinner—though on the quiet side. She'd caught him examining her intently several times. Once she'd even offered him a penny for his thoughts, but he'd just smiled, said they weren't worth that much, and asked her if she lived in New York City. His question required that she indulge in some quick thinking as she danced around a straight answer.

A nurdle of guilt ate at her. She should tell him the truth. Now that she knew him a little better, she *wanted* to tell him, but the truth would spoil the evening. She couldn't remember when she'd enjoyed herself more, and her time with him would come to an end soon. No point in ruining what was for her a fairy-tale moment in time—Cinderella and her Prince Charming. She'd cherish the memory of this night—always.

Adam joined her, one arm over the back of the loveseat almost touching her, the other holding his drink. "I'm glad you didn't mind that I ordered for you. You didn't think the Cornish game hen and dressing too unsophisticated?"

"I thought it was the perfect holiday dinner. The food reminded me of Christmas gatherings at home with a twenty-pound turkey and all the trimmings." Dallas sipped at her brandy and tucked her bare legs more securely under her butt. She snuggled further into the corner of the loveseat, her hair piled on the top of her head, a St. Regis bathrobe—identical to the one Adam wore—wrapped and belted around her. She fiddled with the tie as their conversation hit a lull. She glanced up and caught him *looking* at her again over the rim of a brandy snifter as he sipped the gold liquid.

Was he waiting for her to leave? What *was* the protocol for this sort of thing? She glanced at the clock. Five minutes to midnight. As much as she hated the idea of going to her lonely suite, she was pretty certain "gifts" weren't supposed to sleep over. He probably was just being polite and waiting for her to get the hint. With a true pang of regret, she unfolded from the couch, stood, and placed her brandy snifter on the coffee table. As he watched, she began to pick up her clothes, draping them over her arm in preparation for putting them back on. She cleared her throat, pasted a smile on her face and turned to him. "I had a lovely evening, but I think I should get dressed and be on my way. Ah…thank you again for the—"

He stood abruptly. "I don't want you to leave. Spend tonight and tomorrow with me? I'm sure working Christmas wasn't part of the arrangement, but—"

"Yes." She beamed at him. "Yes, I'll stay the night and yes, I'll spend Christmas with you."

"That was easy." He laughed. "I've been racking my brain to think of what to say to entice you to stay."

She rolled her eyes. "It's pretty hard to ignore two orgasms and apple pie with vanilla ice cream." His gaze held hers and radiated pleasure. She stood not three feet from him and grinned like an idiot.

His face wore a similar expression before he pursed his lips and looked down, suddenly serious. "I supposed we should get this out of the way." He glanced up. "What is your per diem?" A smile tugged at the corners of his mouth. "Other than orgasms and pie."

"My per diem?" *Ah, yes.* She was supposed to be a working girl. She sobered and held his direct gaze. "Christmas is my personal time. I choose how and with whom I spend it. As of midnight, I'm off the clock, so to speak."

"I'm honored that you will spend your time with me."

She shrugged and threw him a mischievous glance. "You should be. I'm very, very expensive."

He arched an eyebrow. "Then get that very, very expensive ass in my bed."

~*~

Theo sauntered after her as Eve scampered down the hallway toward the master bedroom. After a momentary detour in the ensuite bathroom—there was an item or two he wanted from one of the cabinets—he sat next to where she lay nude on the disordered bed. The soft velvet of her cheek met his forefinger as he drew it down her make-up free face. God, she was gorgeous—a lovely combination of demure yet bold femininity. What would she make of what he was going to propose? "I wish I knew you better."

Her eyes widened, and she cocked her head in question at his statement.

With a soft laugh, he held up a pair of broad, padded, leather cuffs studded with rings. Each cuff trailed a foot of light chain with clips on the ends. Her mouth made a silent "O."

"I want to tie you to the bed and tease you until you beg me to fuck you... but I don't know you well enough to suggest such a thing."

For a long moment, she stared at him, her blue-eyed gaze spiked with mischief, then stretched out her arms. "Put them on. I'd like you to know me better."

He buckled a cuff around each wrist. "And you won't mind if I make you beg?"

She met his direct stare. "I don't think I'll mind anything you do."

With a bark of laughter, he swept her up in his arms and rolled onto his back on the bed, pulling her on top of him. "What a sweetheart you are. You truly aren't worried? You can call someone if you want."

She shook her head, amusement playing across her face. "Curious and aroused... not concerned."

"Well then... " He flipped them again and straddled her waist. The fine chains from the cuffs clipped easily around the spindle headboard. He left the chains loose. He wanted her to have enough slack to move her arms—a little.

A slight lean to the left brought the bedside chest within reach, and he pulled open the second drawer and considered the contents. A relaxed and silent Dallas watched him intently. "I think this will do." He held up a pink plastic butterfly with black elastic bands and smiled at the recognition on her face. "And this, too, I think." He tossed a remote control to the bed and moved to kneel between her legs. "Ever use one of these vibrators?"

"I've looked at them in online catalogs. I've never bought one."

"Innocent enough looking, but the new versions can be programmed for quite a diabolical tease. Lift your hips, please." He tossed her a quick grin as he adjusted the black elastic to hold the butterfly securely in place over her clit and then turned it on. The intermittent, variable pulse created a soft hum that ranged from low to high, broken by inconsistent periods of silence.

"Oh…my…that could…mmm." Her eyes closed and her hips undulated in a subtle motion he wasn't sure even *she* was aware of.

"Now that I'm sure you will be entertained, I'm going to spend some time playing with my Christmas gift."

Her eyelids slid half open, and she observed him blissfully. "Color me entertained. Let the games begin."

He chuckled. "Yes…well, God forbid you should be bored."

Her low laughter was answer enough as he lay on his side next to her and teased a rose-pink nipple into a hard bud and then suckled, enjoying her gasps of appreciation as his tongue repeatedly flicked the tip of her nipple. He pressed his nose into the soft, yielding flesh of her breast and reveled in her clean feminine scent. It was no wonder to him men were breast-oriented. Those soft globes fed his fascination, and the moans of appreciation from the woman underneath made him root more urgently and press his hard cock into the satin of her upper thigh.

His free hand left her breast and trailed down her side to cup her buttock and pull her forcefully into him. He groaned as her warm flesh pressed on his, applying pressure where he wanted it the most. Only his personal sense of dignity kept him from humping her leg like a dog. The action also ground the pink butterfly harder between his partner's legs and her writhing intensified.

"Oh…oh…oh god…oh god…I'm gonna…oooh, gawd!"

Her soft cry of ultimate pleasure almost sent him over.

He pulled off her nipple with a hard suck and rested his head on her sternum, dragging huge inhales through his nose and exhaling in blasts through his mouth. He loosened the grip he'd maintained on her soft butt cheek and allowed her to sink to the bed. With a quick flick of the remote control, the low hum of the vibrator stopped.

"Damn, Eve…there are times I distinctly regret being a gentleman." He raised his gaze to hers and answered the question in her eyes. "If I weren't, I'd spread your legs like a wishbone and fuck you through the wall."

She blinked like a deer in the headlights, then her expression morphed into amusement, and she spread her legs wide. "Bring it on, cowboy. Fuck me through the wall."

Without thought, he grabbed one of the black and gold squares from the bedside table, wrapped himself and knelt between Eve's thighs, hoisting her knees over his shoulders. Centering the head of his cock in her wet folds, he hilted himself, his fingers denting the soft flesh of her ass. His head fell back, and he groaned from the pulses of erotic sensation ripping through him as her hot flesh gripped his cock. He drove into her with full, measured strokes that hit the end of her each time. He supposed in the future when he thought back to this moment, he might be ashamed at how selfishly—and forcefully—he rutted on her, but he doubted it.

Twenty minutes later, made boneless from one of the more memorable orgasms in his life, he collapsed onto Eve's chest. "You okay?" he muttered into her soft breast.

"Mmm...yeaahh," she murmured. "Better than okay."

"I didn't do a thing for you."

A soft snort preceded her whisper. "You weren't paying attention then."

Silence surrounded them as he tried to decode her meaning. It took him longer than normal as most of his blood was still below the waist, and stunning pleasure had hornswoggled his brain. He still wasn't certain he'd understood for he *hadn't* been paying attention to her. He'd been too lost in his own pleasure. He fumbled for her wrists and unbuckled the cuffs.

She shifted her arms down to her sides and then stroked his lower back. "I learned something about myself today."

"Ummm?"

"I can come just from penetration."

He lifted his head and peered at her blearily through one eye. "What? So...ah...you...ah..." He fumbled for words.

A wide grin stretched the corners of her mouth. "Yeah." Satisfaction saturated her voice.

Good. That was good. That meant he wasn't an unfeeling, selfish douche. Eyes closed, limbs loose, he forced himself to kneel and then looked down at her. "Be right back." Stripping and discarding the condom, he stumbled to the bathroom and turned on the hot water, plopping a washcloth in the sink. He cleaned himself, rinsed it out and grabbed a fresh washcloth which he saturated with hot water, rang out and then carried into the bedroom for Eve. He sat on the side of the bed while she gingerly wiped between her legs.

"Thanks."

She extended the damp cloth to him, and he tossed it onto the marble floor in the bathroom and then climbed into the bed next to her, shoving the used and unused sex toys onto the floor. Slinging an arm around her waist, he pulled her to him and settled into her plush body. Damn she felt good.

She purred a happy sigh and whispered, "Good night, Adam. I'm looking forward to Christmas with you."

"Good night, Eve. Sweet dreams."

What was it about this woman? There was something about her that eased him. He let down his guard with her as he hadn't done with another woman in … oh, lord… he couldn't remember. He supposed knowing she wasn't a professional had something to do with it. He was curious to see how she would handle her departure. He didn't think she had an agenda. He wanted to believe that their meeting was serendipity, but time would resolve that issue. He was teased by the thought his emotions were…invested… in the outcome. *Interesting.*

ST REGIS
NEW YORK

Chapter Five

Dallas drowsed between sleep, and awake—that lovely never-never land of total relaxation where the body luxuriates in serene bliss and the mind is not yet awake enough to belabor her with things to do, places to go and people to see. The images of a few words danced and twirled through her consciousness as if petals thrown by flower girls. *Theo Stockard. !Amazing! Sex.* A secret smile played at the edges of her mouth. The Spanish punctuation seemed appropriate for that description. The Mormon Tabernacle Choir singing *Amazing Sex* in six-part harmony wouldn't have been out of place.

She supposed she should make some attempt to rise. It was Christmas Day after all. What time was it? She didn't need to look to know she was alone in the big bed. She moaned and rolled over, hugging the pillow closer to her, dragging another one over her head, unwilling to abandon sleep. She'd always had difficulty waking up…nothing had changed as she grew older.

The tantalizing smell of coffee seduced her into opening her eyes. Not six inches in front of her nose, a silver tray sat on the bedside table. On it, a fine china cup on a pretty saucer steamed with the aroma of the elixir of the gods—coffee. Coffee was perhaps the only thing that could roust her from the warm nest of her bed. She sat up against the headboard, the silk sheet maintaining her modesty—but only just—and sipped her coffee, holding the cup between her hands like a supplicant at Holy Communion.

Theo sauntered in looking all too fine in dark slacks, black leather belt, white pima cotton dress shirt rolled to his elbows and barefoot. With a slow grin that did wicked things to her, he sat on her side of the bed.

"Merry Christmas."

She cocked her head sideways, cleared her throat and blinked flirtatiously. "Merry Christmas to you, too."

"Hungry?" With feather light touch, his finger traced her left nipple until it hardened into a prominent nubbin poking the silk of the white sheet.

Gooseflesh covered her arms—an outward sign of the far more devastating effect his touch had elsewhere. She shivered and put her coffee on the table rather than spill it. "Starving, now that you mention it."

"I've ordered brunch. Room service should be here in a few minutes. Thought I'd give you the option of eating it hot…" he grinned "…or cold." He leaned forward and took her mouth with his. The hand that had teased her breast cupped the back of her head and held her into a long, tantalizing kiss of soft lips and exploring tongue.

"Mmm…" Her eyes closed briefly, and she licked her lips when he broke away. "What time is it?"

"1:30 or thereabouts."

"What!" She straightened. The sheet fell to her waist. "Why did you let me sleep so late?"

His head fell back as he laughed. His eyes remained lit with devilment as he leveled them on her. "I tried to wake you—but short of a bucket of water, you weren't surrendering your covers. Tsk, tsk." He wagged his finger at her. "Such language."

Slow heat rose up her chest to her neck and then scalded her cheeks. Even with no memory of it, she could reconstruct exactly what had happened. She groaned and slid down, pulling the sheet over her head. "Sorry." She allowed the sheet to slip to her chin. "I grew up with four fiends from the depths of hell who plagued my existence. My mother claimed them, so I guess that made them my brothers. I learned to fight back early on. In my defense, I shouldn't be held accountable for things I say in my sleep."

"Okay." Theo chuckled. "As long as you don't see *me* in a brotherly light."

"No! Good god, no!" A very unladylike snort erupted from her. She clapped her hand over her mouth at the sound and eyed him.

Shaking his head, Theo grinned broadly. "And that, ladies and gentlemen, was as genuine a response as you'll ever hear." He reached forward and tugged a lock of her hair. "I'm going to make an executive decision. Get up. Slip on a robe. Brush your teeth, whatever, and have brunch with me." As he stood, he leaned down and placed a soft kiss on her lips. "If the food isn't enough reason, I have a surprise for you."

"You, alone, are enough reason …but what's the surprise?"

He nodded in acceptance of her compliment and lifted a negligent shoulder with a smile. "You'll have to see for yourself."

~*~

Dallas snuggled into her white satin wrap lined with white qiviut and fingered the diamond drop that nestled in her décolleté—a four-karat stone that was *not* faux. The jewel was suspended from a dainty diamond and emerald necklace and rested above a gorgeous Prada LBD—little black dress—all gifts from Theo. From inside his sleek, black limousine, she watched the Christmas lights of New York harbor pass. Brilliant, multi-colored lights festooned the boats in the harbor and added to the festive holiday feeling. This evening…shoot, the entire *day* after she'd sauntered into the suite's dining room at a bright and early 2:30 in the afternoon…had been pulled from some romantic fantasy.

Theo pulled her closer to his side and rested his chin briefly on her head. "Did you enjoy *Hamilton*?"

She pulled back enough to look at his handsome face, or what she could see of it in the dark vehicle. "Immensely. The seats were excellent. Thank you so much for taking me. I don't know how you got tickets to it. I've been trying for ages, and it's always sold out."

"Hmm…sometimes you just have to know the right people. I'm glad you enjoyed it."

She settled back into his warmth with a low purr. "I've loved every minute of this day. You've made me feel like Cinderella at the ball—an elegant gown, a romantic dinner at the River Café and a Broadway show." She sighed. "You definitely qualify as Prince Charming. I'm going to hate to return to normal life. When you surprise a girl, you don't mess around."

He made some inarticulate response, and they lapsed into comfortable silence.

During that afternoon and all throughout dinner she'd been entertained, challenged and amused by Theo's topics of conversation. It was as if he was exploring her brain for insight into her character and she felt she'd held her own. Without giving too much away about what she really did for a living, they'd had a lively exchange about the viability of real estate as a long-term investment and the prospects for redeveloping abandoned city-center properties into parks and residential housing. He'd surprised her with his ambitions to give back to the communities that supported him so profitably. The two of them had much in common in that respect. Both of them were self-made and raised with a sense of obligation to make their world better than they found it. Under different circumstances, she'd make an effort to get to know this man. She liked him. *Why kid myself?* She more than liked him.

As the car slowly drove the broad New York avenues, the streetlamps and bright lights of the surrounding high-rises cast almost a daytime brightness to the outside and she drank in the sights of holiday revelers, laughing as they walked along the snow-covered city streets. "You didn't have to do all that, you know," she murmured. "We could have stayed in and simply talked…or, ah…whatever." She felt his shrug in the dark.

"I know. We'll get to the 'whatever'." His quiet chuckle vibrated against her side. "It gave me great pleasure to see your undisguised enjoyment of the dress, the jewelry, the show. I don't often get to spread happiness." He paused for a long moment. "My business acquisitions usually result in quite the opposite effect."

"That bothers you?"

"Yes."

From his clipped answer, she'd hit a sore spot, and for the first time since she'd walked into Theo's suite, she felt she'd trespassed somehow. She knew the man donated heavily to a long list of charitable organizations, everything from NPRA to the ASPCA and Red Cross, but he'd also been responsible for the breakup of large conglomerates with the resulting layoffs of thousands of employees. On the flip side, he'd financed re-education programs for older workers then helped place them in permanent employment. "Select Services, Inc.," the organization he founded, was considered one of the vanguard examples for how to deal with an aging workforce possessing obsolete skills. Of course, she couldn't allude to any of that, so instead, she pulled his arm closer around her, raised his hand to her lips and kissed his knuckles. "Thank you for a magical evening. I'll never forget it."

"It's not over yet, Eve. You'll stay until tomorrow."

She wasn't certain if he'd asked a question or given an order, but she treated it like a question. "Yes, sir. I have to leave in the morning, but it would be my pleasure to stay until then."

~*~

Back in the palatial suite, she slipped out of her designer gown, put her necklace back in the navy blue velvet Harry Winston box, removed her makeup, and brushed her hair out of the upsweep she'd worn for the theater. She shrugged into the terrycloth robe provided by the St. Regis—a robe she'd already determined was going to leave with her as a memento of this weekend. She examined herself in the bathroom mirror and took a deep breath. The fairytale was coming to an end. Her heart ached, and her eyes smarted with unshed tears when she thought about getting on that plane tomorrow, knowing she'd never see him again. Theo Stockard was a thoroughly wonderful man, and she would have killed for the opportunity to meet him under different circumstances—circumstances that would have allowed for the possibility of more permanence than a three day weekend. He liked her, and she liked him—too much, but she'd put herself between and rock and a hard spot. She couldn't confess to her real identity. He'd throw her out on her ass—and deservedly so. She'd lied to him. In a moment of willful selfishness, she'd lied to and used Theo and then perpetuated her crime by staying longer than she should have. It was in her best interests to ensure they never met again, and the thought filled her with unexpected sadness.

She straightened and pasted a determined smile on her face. She didn't have to be on the plane to Dallas until 11:00 tomorrow morning. If this was all the time she had left with him, she'd make the most of it.

Her bare feet made little sound as she padded into the living room and stopped. The only light in the room came from a fire in the fireplace. Theo stood pensively at a picture window looking out onto Central Park and sipped scotch. He'd taken off his suit jacket and loosened his tie, but otherwise wore the same clothes he'd had on all evening. He must have heard her, for he turned and smiled. "I didn't think you could look more exquisite than you did this evening... but I was wrong. I find I like you just as well barefoot and in a bathrobe as in Prada and diamonds."

"Thank you."

"You're welcome." He opened his arms, and she walked into them. He gathered her to him and placed a kiss on her forehead before turning and looking out the window again, holding her snuggled under his shoulder, his arm around her waist.

"Look," she whispered, mesmerized by the fat flakes that floated by the window and gave each light outside a halo. "It's snowing. How beautiful."

"Yes, it is, isn't it? I'd forgotten just how beautiful." He took a small sip from his tumbler. "You've reminded me of many things I'd forgotten."

"Good things, I hope."

"Hmm…for the most part. Being with you this weekend has brought home to me how lonely I've been. My friends are right. I've been working too hard for too long, and it took a warm, intelligent woman to remind me just what's lacking in my life." His eyes found hers in the dark room, and there was no mistaking the admiration and desire in his gaze.

She swallowed her imminent tears. She refused to recognize the emotion welling in her heart, for it was the height of foolishness to have fallen so hard on such a short acquaintance—an acquaintance built on deception. She'd give anything to go back thirty-six hours and start again. She blessed the darkness for hiding the tremble in her smile. "Please don't take anymore gifts from Charlie. You are a fine man. You just need to give yourself a chance to meet the right woman. She's out there." The knowledge that she'd doomed any prospect that it could have been her had her blinking rapidly and clearing her throat.

"Well, I have a fabulous woman in my arms, right now, and I'm going to enjoy her thoroughly." He placed his tumbler on the marble window sill, caught her under her knees, and lifted her up.

She wrapped her arms around his neck and laughed softly as he carried her in long strides down the hallway and laid her on the turned down bed. Sitting beside her, he pulled off his shoes and socks, stripped off his trousers and briefs and then began work on the buttons of his shirt.

She sighed in appreciation. "You are *such* a pretty man."

"Glad someone appreciates the hours in the gym. Now, out of that robe."

She closed her eyes and tried to memorize the feel of his hard, warm body pressed against hers, the gentle kisses he pressed to her torso and breasts and neck and lips…the sensation of his wet mouth suckling her breasts while his talented fingers found the wet folds between her legs and drove her mindless with arousal. She tried to commit to memory the exquisite sensation of fullness as he slid his hard cock into her, and how she screamed with joy when she could no longer stand the erotic torture and orgasm rocked her body. She never wanted to forget the long hours of this night as he made love to her over and over again until human flesh simply surrendered to earthly limits.

Chapter Six

It was still dark when she tip-toed out of the bedroom in the early morning hours while Theo slept. She hadn't trusted herself to wake in time and so spent the last hour or so simply watching him and wiping away the tears that trickled down her cheeks. In spite of the ache centered in her chest, she'd do it again in a heartbeat. She couldn't bear the thought of having to face him, so she'd made her escape as silently as possible. Sometime during the past twenty-four hours, the invisible butler service had removed the clothing she'd arrived in, had them cleaned and pressed and returned to the suite. She simply sighed in silent appreciation and put them on.

She'd left him a thank you note—and the necklace. She'd taken the dress and the wrap.

A confused bell captain put her bags in a black town car while she signed her receipt for a palatial suite she'd never used and one bathrobe.

"Where to, madam?"

"La Guardia, please."

***

He heard the soft chime of the doorbell to the suite and a feminine voice call out, "Housekeeping, sir." Another soft rap followed closely. "Housekeeping, Mr. Stockard." He glanced at the bedside clock. *Shit!* He'd overslept—by hours. He'd meant to wake up early and have an honest discussion with Dallas. He propped himself up on his elbows, immediately aware he was alone in the room. *Shit, shit, shit!* Naked, he threw the sheet back, padded into the bathroom and grabbed a robe, donning it while striding down the hallway toward the living room and the entry hall. "Eve? You still here? Eve?" His voice echoed in the empty suite. "God damn it." And then he saw the thank you note propped against the blue jewelry case on the coffee table. He flipped it open and scanned the flowing black script on the heavy card stock. "God-*damn-it*, Dallas."

His head dropped back, and he stood staring at the ceiling, his hands on his hips, thinking… *feeling*. He'd always gone with his "gut" in business, and this acquisition would be no different. He didn't know if she was "the one," but he sure as hell wanted the opportunity to find out. He walked to the sideboard in the hallway and pulled out the drawer where he'd hidden her phone. It was still there. The screen displayed an alert for an American flight to Dallas/Ft. Worth departing La Guardia that morning. He could get there in time if he chartered a helicopter. A smile grew across his face. Miss Dallas Hutchinson wasn't walking out of his life so easily.

He nodded at the neatly uniformed young woman who entered. "Please come back in thirty minutes, and I'll be out of your hair."

***

She felt like a zombie, both from sheer fatigue and emotional upheaval. A time would come—a month, perhaps two—when she'd remember this weekend and be able to grin from ear to ear, but right now her smile wobbled a bit. There was nothing worse than having a bad case of "what might have been." The time until her flight departure seemed to grind on, particularly since she didn't have the distraction of her phone. She didn't know what had happened to it. She'd thought it was in her purse... but it must have fallen out somewhere. Quite possible, as she'd been on the ragged edge of tears and mentally scattered trying to leave as quickly and quietly as possible.

Finally, they announced the call for first class boarding, and she settled into her seat and fastened her seat belt. Opening the goody bag that the airlines gave their first class passengers, she removed the eye mask and blanket and settled in for a good three hours rest. She kept her fingers crossed that no one would sit in the seat next to her and it seemed she was in luck. She remained alone in her row. *Halleluia.* She could let sleep soothe her wounded heart and not have to make trite conversation with some horny businessman.

As the plane began to push back, the pilot came on and announced they were returning to the gate. Eve registered the peculiar announcement but snuggled further into her blanket and concentrated on trying to sleep. She vaguely recognized the sounds of the hatch being opened and the flight attendant speaking with someone and then Eve felt her seat shake as a large body slid into the space next to her. *Damn.* She hunched toward the window and moved the blanket up to cover her face.

"May I bring you something to drink before takeoff, sir?"

"Yes, I'll have a scotch, neat. Thank you."

Her breath caught. She knew that voice. She *knew* that voice! Her heart began to pound like to escape her chest, and she straightened in her seat one vertebra at a time. She pulled off the eye mask, ran her fingers through her hair, took a steadying breath—and turned to face him. *Wicked man.*

Theo gave her a crooked smile as his eyes roamed her face. She met his direct gaze and returned his smile, while a thousand thoughts gyrated through her mind like a cluster of feral cats in a burlap sack.

His eyes lit up with devilry, and he extended his hand. "Hello. I don't believe we've met. I'm Theo Stockard."

She fought to keep from wriggling in her seat with delight and a small laugh of sheer happiness escaped. She placed her hand in his. "I'm pleased to meet you, Mr. Stockard. I'm Dallas Hutchinson."

His grip was firm and didn't let go, and her smile widened to a full-on grin when he raised her captive hand to his mouth and in a very old-fashioned gesture, kissed it. His eyes softened with an emotion she didn't dare give a name to.

"When did you know?" she asked.

With an enigmatic lift of eyebrows, he reached into his suit coat. "Here, I believe this belongs to you." In his extended hand was her phone.

She took the phone. "You've known from the first, you devil." She caught her lip between her teeth and shook her head in a mock scold, but its effect was minimized by her chirp of laughter and the fact she couldn't stop beaming.

His handsome face smiled back at her, giving nothing away.

"Are you going to Dallas on business or pleasure, Mr. Stockard?" she teased.

He tucked her hand into his as if he had no intention of ever releasing her. "Please call me, Theo. Pleasure, Ms. Hutchinson, definitely pleasure."

The ~~End~~ Beginning

Other Books by Patricia A. Knight

Hers to Command

For some, existence without their mate might seem like the end of their world... for the Verdantia's Tetriarch, it would be.

Conte Camliel Aristos deTano, Ari, has long spurned the marriage forced upon him. His contractual bride, Princess Fleur Constante, the beautiful future queen though young and inexperienced, is willing to risk everything, including her own sanity, to save her planet.

The inhabitants of the sentient planet, Verdantia, are poised on the precipice of extinction following a brutal invasion by an off-world, nomadic horde. Verdantia's capital, Sylvan Mintoth, must have its failing energy shield restored, or the planet is doomed. The Elders know the shield can draw energy from only one thing- a very arduous and grueling coupling of two specific people who were pre-chosen by the planet Herself and promised by prearranged marriage contract.

Verdantia draws strength from the duo, but the sentient planet whispers to Ari that a third is necessary ~ Ari's aide de camp, Visconte Doral deLorion, an angelically handsome, skilled assassin who silently surrendered his heart to Ari long ago.

The trio struggles to make this surprising partnership harmonious, pushing through pride, scars of past abuse, fears of inexperience and distrust. To save Verdantia, they must overcome their individual weaknesses and realize their full potential. Only the tetriarch and their combined synergy, can harness Verdantia's immense power to shield its citizens from invasion.

Other Books by Patricia A. Knight

An Evidence of Magic

An Evidence of Magic—69K M/M procedural crime romance in an alternate reality.

Forty-year-old, hard bitten, foul-mouthed, homicide detective, Hiro Santos, suspects the owner of the art studio committed the gory killing. Too bad. There are other things he'd like to do to the gorgeous young man than book him for murder. Worse, his sexy suspect is certifiable. The nutcase claims he's some kind of high wizard from an alternate reality and needs Hiro's help to save their worlds.

While the striking Sable Campion appears a youthful twenty-five, he's endured over two-hundred lonely years as guardian of the portal between Everlight and Elysium. None of those centuries offered him any experience finding a vicious killer. That's where Hiro Santos comes in; but convincing the virile detective to trust Sable will take all his persuasive skills...and perhaps a bit of magic.

The magic they find in each other's arms will rock each of their realities.

About Patricia A. Knight

Patricia A. Knight is the pen name for an eternal romantic who lives in Dallas, Texas surrounded by her horses, dogs and the best man on the face of the earth – oh yeah, and the most enormous bullfrogs you will ever see. Word to the wise: don't swim in the pool after dark.

I love to hear from my readers and can be reached at http://www.patriciaaknight.com. Send me an email at patriciaknight190@gmail.com.

Made in the USA
Lexington, KY
23 January 2018